When I
Grow Up

SEAN COVEY
Illustrated by Stacy Curtis

Ready-to-Read

Simon Spotlight
New York   London   Toronto   Sydney   New Delhi

To my daughter Allie, my little princess,
who I never want to grow up.
—Sean Covey

For Charles Schulz, who gave me
an end in mind.
—Stacy Curtis

SIMON SPOTLIGHT
An imprint of Simon & Schuster Children's Publishing Division
1230 Avenue of the Americas, New York, New York 10020
This Simon Spotlight edition November 2019
Copyright © 2009 by Franklin Covey Co.
For information about special discounts for bulk purchases, please contact Simon & Schuster
Special Sales at 1-866-506-1949 or business@simonandschuster.com.
Manufactured in the United States of America 0719 LAK
2 4 6 8 10 9 7 5 3 1
Library of Congress Cataloging-in-Publication Data
Names: Covey, Sean, author. | Curtis, Stacy, illustrator.
Title: When I grow up / by Sean Covey ; illustrated by Stacy Curtis.
Description: First Simon Spotlight paperback edition. | New York : Simon Spotlight, 2019. | Series:
Ready-to-read. Level 2 | Series: The 7 habits of happy kids ; 2 | Originally published by
Simon & Schuster Books for Young Readers in 2009. | Summary: After her grandmother reads her a
story about growing up, Allie the mouse imagines what she will be like when she is grown.
Includes note to parents and discussion questions.
Identifiers: LCCN 2019017116 | ISBN 9781534444478 (paperback) | ISBN 9781534444485 (hardcover) |
ISBN 9781534444492 (eBook)
Subjects: | CYAC: Growth—Fiction. | Imagination—Fiction. | Bedtime—Fiction. | Mice—Fiction. | BISAC:
JUVENILE FICTION / Readers / Beginner. | JUVENILE FICTION / Imagination & Play. | JUVENILE FICTION /
Social Issues / Self-Esteem & Self-Reliance.
Classification: LCC PZ7.C8343 Wh 2019 | DDC [E]—dc23
LC record available at https://lccn.loc.gov/2019017116

Tagalong Allie
was very sleepy.
It was time
to go to bed.

Allie snuggled
under her covers.

Her granny read her a story.
It was about a little girl
who grew up.

Granny finished the story.
She gave Allie a kiss.

"Time to go to sleep,"
said Granny.
She turned off the light.

After Granny left,
Allie lay wide awake.

Allie sat up.
She looked at the moon
outside her window.
"When I get bigger," said Allie,
"I want to grow up too."
She imagined what it would be like
to be all grown up.

She could wear
lots of makeup.

She would have
lots of jewelry.

She could get dressed up
and go to fancy parties.

She would walk to the grocery store
all by herself.
She would shop for food.

She would make
yummy cakes.

Allie could write
her very own book.

Then she would go to work
at her very own pizza shop!

Allie and her friends would
hike to a waterfall.

Someday she might even fly
to the moon.

But first Allie needed to
go to school.

She would
do her chores.

And she needed to
go to sleep.
Then she could grow up.

Allie turned over,
closed her eyes,
and fell sound asleep.

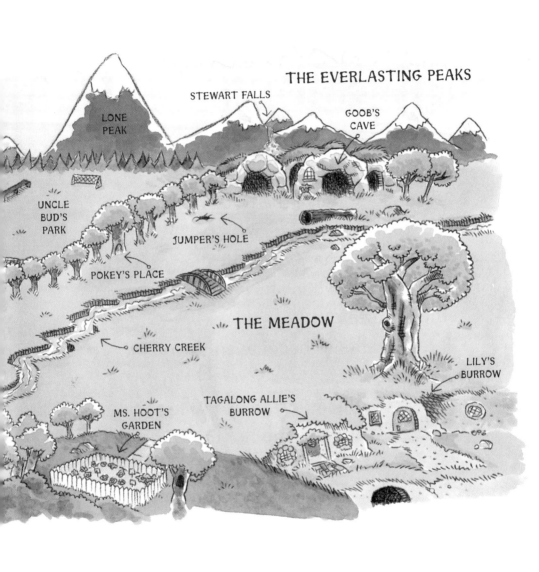

Up for Discussion

1. What story did Granny tell Allie at bedtime?

2. What are some of the things Allie would like to do when she grows up? Where will she work? What book will she write? How will she feel when she hikes to the top of the waterfall?

3. If Allie wants to become an astronaut someday, what does she need to do?

4. Why is it still important for Allie to brush her teeth and pick up her toys if her dreams are so much more fun?

5. What do you want to be when you grow up? What will you do? Where will you live? How will you feel? How are you going to get there?

Baby Steps

1. Let's set a timer for thirty seconds. In thirty seconds, tell your mommy or daddy all the things you want to do when you grow up. On your mark, get set, go. . . .
2. Now set that timer for thirty seconds again. This time, tell your mommy or daddy all the work you need to do to reach your dreams someday. On your mark, get set, go. . . .
3. Open up a fun family magazine. Get a pen and circle all the fun activities, places, and people that you see. Show them to a friend.
4. Draw a picture of how you will look when you are all grown up. Use lots of colors.
5. Hang a piece of paper on the wall in your bedroom. Every time you think of something new you'd like to do when you grow up, have your big sister or brother or parents help you write it down.

PARENTS' CORNER

HABIT ② — Begin with the End in Mind: *Have a Plan*

I remember tucking my own Allie into bed one night when she told me about all the things she wanted to do when she grew up, like have a baby, drive a car, and make yummy food, hopefully not in that order. I was impressed with how well she could picture the future at the mere age of three. Children are blessed with the gift of imagination, which is one of the four gifts that make us human, along with conscience, self-awareness, and willpower. And we should do all we can to nurture imagination, not smother it. After all, this is what beginning with the end in mind is all about. It's about visualizing the end state you want, whether it be in a job, a relationship, or a feeling, and then working to achieve it. All things are created twice, you see. First in the mind's eye . . . then for real. Just ask Helen Keller, Mahatma Gandhi, Superman, or Cinderella.

In this story, highlight how Allie begins with the end in mind. She imagines how much fun it will be to grow up and shop, cook, hike, and even fly. She creates this future in her mind's eye in vivid detail. But she then realizes that to get what she wants tomorrow, she must do the little things today, like doing her chores, brushing her teeth, and going to bed.